Worried
Little Lamb

Valérie Guidoux
Adapted by Patricia Jensen
Illustrations by Philippe Poirier

Reader's Digest Kids
Pleasantville, N.Y.—Montreal

One fine day, all the sheep were going to the meadow in the valley to graze on the new spring grass. "Come along," Mother called to Little Lamb, who was playing with some butterflies. "It's time for your first trip to the valley."

"I'm coming," said Little Lamb.

The mischievous Woodchuck was hiding nearby and heard their conversation.

"Little Lamb is going to the valley for the first time," he chuckled. "I know how my friend Rabbit and I can have some fun."

Woodchuck called to Little Lamb. "My friend Rabbit and I have been to the valley many times. To get there, you must climb down a very steep cliff. Poor Little Lamb! You'll never be able to do it."

"Why not?" she asked.

"Well, your legs aren't strong enough," said Woodchuck. "You'll probably stumble and tumble all the way to the bottom."

Little Lamb was very young and believed almost everything she heard.

"Oh, my," said Little Lamb, her eyes wide with fright.

Little Lamb raced after the flock of sheep and found Grandma.

"Grandma," she asked. "Do I have to climb down a cliff to get to the valley?"

"Yes, you do," answered Grandma.

"Oh, no," Little Lamb said in a shaky voice. "I won't make it down that cliff. My legs aren't strong enough."

Grandma smiled. "You won't know until you try, Little Lamb. Besides, your mother certainly wouldn't lead you to a place you couldn't reach. We will all be there to help you."

But Little Lamb was still worried when she caught up to Grandpa.

"Grandpa," she said, "I am afraid that my legs are too weak to carry me down the cliff."

Grandpa snorted. "Your legs are plenty strong enough. You'll have no trouble at all. Besides, your mother and grandmother and I will be there to help you."

Little Lamb finally arrived at the edge of the cliff. Some of the sheep were resting before climbing down to the valley. Others had already started down. Little Lamb peered over the side.

"Oh, no!" she thought. "This cliff is much too steep. Woodchuck and Rabbit were right—I will never be able to climb down! I'll stumble and tumble all the way to the bottom!"

Little Lamb's mother found her daughter and said, "We're almost there."

"But, Mother," cried Little Lamb, "I can't climb down such a steep cliff. My legs are much too weak."

"Where did you ever get that idea?" asked her surprised mother.

"Woodchuck told me," said Little Lamb tearfully. "And Rabbit thinks so, too."

"You'll never know what you can do until you try," Mother said gently. "And we're all here to help you."

Little Lamb's mother began to lead the way. Little Lamb took a deep breath, and then she took one careful step, and another, and another.

Little Lamb climbed all the way down the cliff slowly and carefully. Woodchuck and Rabbit were waiting at the bottom.

Little Lamb's mother went over to the two rascals. "You have been mean to Little Lamb today," she scolded. "You should not have told her that she wouldn't be able to climb down the cliff. It was not too steep for her."

"We were only kidding," said Woodchuck, hanging his head in shame.

"Playing tricks on your friends is not a good way to have fun," Mother said firmly.

"We're sorry," said Woodchuck.

Little Lamb's mother smiled as Little Lamb
played in the meadow with Rabbit, Woodchuck,
and all their brothers and sisters.

"I've learned how to find out things for myself," Little Lamb said to Woodchuck. "So no one will be able to trick me again. And I know now that my legs are strong. In fact, they are so strong, I can give you all a ride!"